MURDER ALIVE !

THE ONLY MISTAKE WHY I LOVE HER

AYAANSH

Some say people time has given
my life in group decision, where
people believe catch my life
as peep to understand me
as laughter shine as people come
as partly shown as
people has given me
understand me Laughter
me as course beauty
to understand to understand,
me as partly shown
8 G.P. to N.D. human man
understand my Sisters
Smith. Slave top within
to renew a charismatic
two where people choice smile
has given Muslim to know who
the said has understand
me to know my life in
grown partly to know me
life short part to know
me love to understand
are as take, have people who
has confused me to
know my life
my pis not a understand my
life in grave mankind
in greater strike.

"Dark morning welcomes you in night crime"...

you inner beauty [illegible]

[illegible] in search of [illegible]
where somebody for very care
for your life [illegible] personal
believe in [illegible]
in [illegible]
[illegible] your [illegible]
find your nostalgic
by somebody [illegible]

[illegible] in [illegible]
[illegible] night [illegible]
[illegible] beauty [illegible]

•This book is dedicated to all mighty creatures" ..

Contents

Preface

This poetry is all about not been thirst for some body else attention in your life . Trust is more valuable thing and you have to maintain the dignity of trust life along.

I believe my character Beauty has defined that how he considered everything is waste accept your definition but he forget in life, definition can be extended till death.

I personally believe in this world until you die you cannot be legend because after death celebration of definition has to be define by some body else .

we don't have to win somebody we have to create inner joy for them in this world and it's impossible. Remember mistake is love but when you understand definition , affection , care , and happiness and you don't want something as reward that is love." which means that "When you become definition for

someone that is love "..

Acknowledgements

I am grateful to all in this cosmos who survive the long pandemic and thank all of you to make this possible. I believe sometimes this pandemic used to speak with us that unity discover the solution of any problem . Last year many of us have lost many creatures , character some have understand their own existence that is why I consider loving somebody with purity doesn't signifies you but knowing your character then coming back to this cosmos then giving love to every creature and taking their treat and affection back at some point of time you have defined your real beauty and then you don't need to struggle for love .

Because the only mistake is "why I loved her " .

1. Murder Alive..

It was slighted as mood of dark

I ignore every time I supposed to be in my special days

those were my best days .

those days were imagination for me .

I was O'nesecutive when rain introduced me

I pray to god each and every day till last day

sudden grief she was roof of my happiness

these mood doesn't go well I recognize my self in me
as new try.

but now time has shown its dawn era

everything I did was right the only mistake is why I loved her

I am not able to conceit myself in new moon.

2. Moon Confession

Moon bar just look at her every time

I always recommend myself to be recognised

My frame is to say a word

You confess first rhyme

A sole understand me as a shower

My prime night to great time

I cry till hours

But I am not happy

I always write about your saints beauty

My eyes recognise you everytime

Coury you don't respect my bless heart

I always rain my eyes into you

My vein , my hope will never die,

Please speak to me

Otherwise my heart will die

Cheer a word to know

Curiosity of your essence mine.

3. Threat of life

A day started with crying tone of my voice

Laughing mood in snow fry

Bringing emotions to my eyes to alone cry

I was shocked to know my life

Laughing in nostalgic awake

Still thinks as a treasure frame

Monsoon crave me to know

How sincere the stars frame

Arguing with beauty tears

Loving my mind in bears

Beak me down in star'om well fears

I know for you it's a fear

Short long hours in surgeon room

Speak to me in derived mood

I died in her heart

I buried in her body

Somebody scold her in school hours

Vein describes her as rose

Fading days shout bars

Tear of body in her prose.

4. Blasting the eile

Blazing the rope of corni jope

Remembering the weil my love

I know my pleasure 'ove

Sometimes it gives me pleasure in acoustic sove

I was in my last moon light

I was afraid of my tears might

Wearing my houring regret fright

I decide sunset of moon in beautiful sunshine

They offer no corner in new start

My beam deviated me last hours

My demise hostile me in phrase great

Emission of conceal force me d'yours

I too remember her in gracing wine

Let me take to your private paradise

Search me in palm and cosmic vein

I too remember my green dein

It hurts me at last when I investigated your heart

I am dying in your vein

Collect me into peaces

When you left me in your heart.

5. Tears Cry

I understand great fear in south block

Making some bribe in sunshine

I make noise

Lemme be loud , make my sprout

Shout in mouth

I missed you in a laughter fine

Exhaled me beauty bushes

Left me in a shaded tears

I did cry in your spheres

Let me dye in a situation of life

Living in a course of mine

Living in a paradise nine

Please let tears cry.........

6. Red Killers

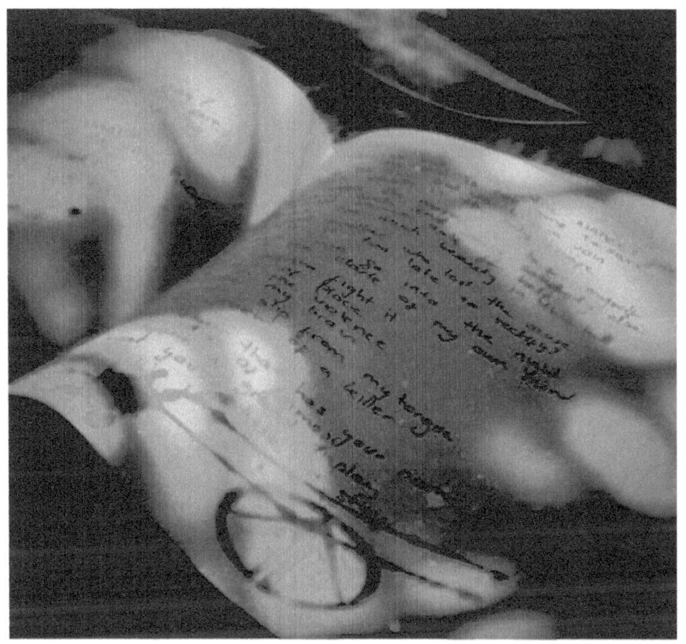

Enter Caption

In loop of sharp

I knotch myself down

Ladders of roof , where lives matter in mirror

our shoes diers.

Lay me down agents ,

aisle of blast my family last

"I had to flee home"

Wars of weaving machine ,

some skin ,some hair, some babies

in crave beeps.

Some papers of immigrants allowed me in ship

The lives in hussle in breif castle

I killed many survivals indeed

emergency naive me down

Bomb blast was something unaware of

Sound was awakening

babies got cheered up

Paradise welcomes us insanely.

7. Dying leaf

Beauty emotion in grasstic phase

understand the pressure in energetic phrase

people died in uncertain dynasty

some understand the beauty of life

reckless beat made me kill in dozen loot

my divergent course where

leaf loves branches

branches loves trees

tree sacrifice life as mist

made a deal understand my nostalgia

phychology deal with care people

I will find my dare

I realise my cause of time

where my mind spears

obstacles tears

I divided myself in eyes and pears

I look in magenta nine

"moon fries"

"sun screams "

"stars shines"

what a tears !

what a cry !

"I believe leaf is dying"

8. Atheist Mind

In life of mine

treasure brime

people frail god in living

moroun in ship

treasure of light got waste

people in sand soil

someone in my brick

Is "LORD" or "FIST"

mighty in centre

creation in invention

minding someone attention

Oh! treasure brime I need to die

allow me to craft

in gesture mark

let me show my heart

in mood of laugh

9. Fell

Where mind is roaming in the sky

fleeting of gold float it on wanton

in coolness of purity transparent smile

white morning held without fear

the vapour of "tea" silence of "sea"

broke into ripples of bird

I was funeral by flowers

we sang no glad songs

nor played violin

we didn't went for village for better

we speak not a word nor smiled

we quickened our pace as

more time speed by

leaves danced, sun smile

we buried ourself and paid no heed

today awaken soul thrill by joy

the pure assence in paid red

"where mind is without fear held high "

Last Words ....

Slightest of the smile in creature mild

A roof of price in everyone life

I deep down circumstantial way where people play

I derived coury oath to revive

majesty life , sun shine , star twinkle , moon light

mesmerizing of people glow in dark salt

exile life of wild in notion devine

harrasing the candy nature

understanding the agression

know to create meaning as lesson

' "LOVE " we cannot prove it

we can only "INTENT" between each other '

• 33 •

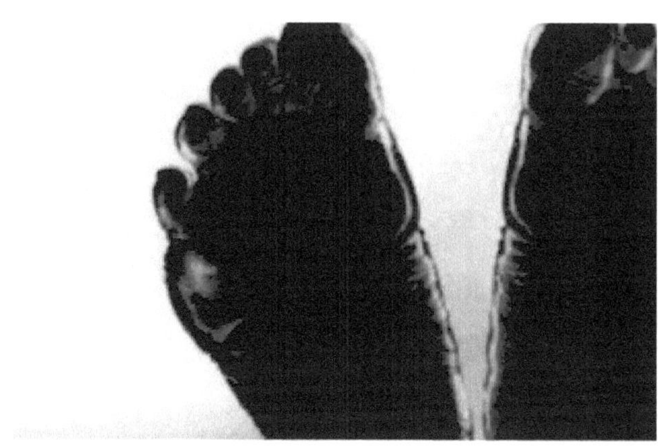

www.ingramcontent.com/pod-product-compliance
Lightning Source LLC
Chambersburg PA
CBHW061407160726
47995CB00001B/499